# The Bears' New Baby

Story and Pictures
by Joan Elizabeth Goodman

For Rio and Deco

A GOLDEN BOOK • NEW YORK
Western Publishing Company, Inc., Racine, Wisconsin 53404

Copyright © 1988 by Joan Elizabeth Goodman. All rights reserved. No part of this book may be reproduced or copied in any form without written permission from the publisher. GOLDEN®, GOLDEN & DESIGN®, A GOLDEN BOOK®, and A LITTLE GOLDEN BOOK® are trademarks of Western Publishing Company, Inc. Library of Congress Catalog Card Number: 87-82392 ISBN: 0-307-03060-1/ISBN: 0-307-60325-3 (lib. bdg.)
CDEFGHIJKLM

One night, after supper, Mama and Papa Bear told Amanda some special news.

"We're going to have a baby!" said Mama.

"You will have a little brother or sister to play with," said Papa.

"Goody!" said Amanda. "When will we get it?"
"The baby will be born in the spring," said Mama.
"When will it be spring?" asked Amanda.
"Soon," said Mama. "Winter is nearly over."

Grandma started coming by in the afternoons so that Mama could nap. Mama's tummy grew bigger and bigger. Amanda could feel the baby move inside.

"It keeps moving around," said Amanda. "I'm going to call it Wiggles."

"Wiggles is a good name for a baby," said Mama. "Let's think of grown-up names, too."

Amanda thought about Wiggles all the time. She felt very sure Wiggles would be a sister. Amanda thought of names for Wiggles. She drew pictures of Wiggles. She thought about how much fun she would have with Wiggles, running, jumping, and playing games.

Many, many days went by.
"Is it spring yet?" asked Amanda.
"Not yet, but soon," said Papa.

One morning Amanda woke up, and Mama and
Papa were gone!

"How could they go away without telling me?" she
asked.

"They had to leave for the hospital in a hurry," said
Grandma. "Your brother, Benjamin, was born late
last night."

"But Wiggles is supposed to be a sister," said
Amanda.

"It's nice to have a brother," said Grandma.
"You'll see."

"When can I see him? And when will Mama come home?" asked Amanda.

"Soon and soon," said Grandma. "Eat your breakfast."

"It seems like it is always *soon*," said Amanda, "and never *now*." She picked at Grandma's oatmeal. It was too lumpy. Even the toast was wrong. It wasn't cut into triangles.

"Nothing is the way it should be," thought Amanda.

Finally Papa came home and told Amanda all about Benjamin and Mama.

"Mama is tired," he said. "But she's very, very happy."

"Doesn't she miss me?" asked Amanda.

"Mama misses you so much," said Papa, "that she and Benjamin are coming home tomorrow."

"Tomorrow!" thought Amanda as she was falling asleep. "There'll be Mama and Papa. And I'll have Wiggles to play with—even if he *is* a brother."

The next day Mama was in her rocking chair when
Amanda came home from school.

"Hello, my little one," she said, giving Amanda a
big hug. "Come and meet your brother."

"*This* is Wiggles?" asked Amanda.

"Yes," said Mama. "His real name is Benjamin, but we will call him Wiggles."

"He's so small and wrinkly," said Amanda.

"When will he be big enough to play with me?" she asked.

"Soon," said Mama. "In the meantime, Wiggles will keep us very busy."

"Wiggles certainly keeps Mama busy," thought Amanda as the days went by. Mama bathed Wiggles, dressed him, fed him, and cleaned him up. She burped him, tickled him, sang to him, and rocked him to sleep. Even so, he cried at night.

"Wiggles is not the kind of baby I wanted," said Amanda. "Couldn't we send him back?"

"No," said Papa. "Besides, soon Wiggles will be bigger and more fun to play with. Then, I think, you will like him very much."

"Soon, hmph!" said Amanda. "I don't think Wiggles will *ever* get bigger or be *any* fun!"

"But he gets bigger all the time!" said Papa. "You must watch him more carefully."

"If he doesn't get bigger or more fun," said Amanda, "then can we send him back?"

"You just keep an eye on him," said Papa.

So from then on, Amanda did watch Wiggles very carefully. He *was* bigger than he had been at first, and fluffier, too. It was nice to cuddle him when he wasn't crying.

Amanda helped Mama feed Wiggles. He got mashed bananas in his ears and peaches on his nose.

"Look how silly he is!" said Amanda.

"Oh, yes!" said Mama. "Wiggles is quite a funny fellow."

One day Amanda was helping Mama dress Wiggles. Mama put a diaper over Wiggles's face, then pulled it away. Wiggles smiled and cooed. "What are you doing?" asked Amanda.

"Wiggles and I are playing peekaboo," said Mama. "Now you try it."

Amanda covered Wiggles with the diaper, then quickly pulled it away. Wiggles giggled. Amanda ducked down out of Wiggles's sight, then popped up.

Wiggles squealed happily. Amanda laughed and laughed. Mama did, too!

"Peekaboo is a good game," said Amanda.

"Wiggles can play lots of good baby games," said Mama. "Some he will teach to us, and some we will teach to him."

At supper that night Amanda said, "Wiggles still isn't the kind of baby I thought we were getting, but he isn't so bad after all."

"I'm glad you think so," said Mama.

"Let's keep him," said Amanda. "But let's get the sister kind, too."

"Perhaps," said Papa.

"Maybe," said Mama.

"When?" asked Amanda.

"Well..." said Mama.
"I know," said Amanda. "It will be *soon*!"
And they all laughed—even Wiggles.